D0886324

# The Last Christmas Cookie

## By Virginia Smith

J.R. Clarke Public Library
102 E. Spring St.
Covington, Ohio  45318

*The Last Christmas Cookie*

© 2011 by Virginia Smith

Published by Next Step Books, P.O. Box 70271, West Valley City, Utah 84170

All rights reserved. No part of this book may be reproduced, stored in a retrieval system, or transmitted in any form or by any means – electronic, mechanical, photocopy, recording, or otherwise – without written permission of the author, except for brief quotations in printed reviews.

Illustrations by MikeMotz.com

Cover Design by MikeMotz.com

Smith, Virginia
The Last Christmas Cookie

ISBN-13: 978-1937671013
ISBN-10: 1937671011

J R Library
10 Spring St
Covington, Ohio 453

For my sister, Susie Smith

Merry Christmas!

Not thoughts of children fast asleep
awaiting Santa without a peep.

Not thoughts of gifts wrapped up below,
nor even Rudolph in the snow.

The only thing my mind could see
was a plate of cookies beneath the tree.

I reasoned, "Surely Santa won't care
if one is missing. He can share!"

So moving as quietly as I dare
I tip-toed swiftly down the stair.

My mind was fixed on a sugary treat
with chocolate chips, deliciously sweet.

Turning the corner I stopped in surprise.
A flash of red clothing caught my eyes.

Right there before my Christmas tree
stood Santa and I saw that he

had in one hand an empty plate.
It appeared as though I was too late.

But then he turned and I chanced to see
in his other hand was the last cookie!

7

He followed my gaze and saw what I wanted.
"Is this what you're after?" he quietly taunted

holding the cookie out like a prize.
I glimpsed a gluttonous gleam in his eyes.

"Now, Santa," I reasoned, "You've had quite a few.
You don't need anymore. I'm just thinking of you."

He considered a moment, and then
licked his lips.
His gaze dropped pointedly
to my hips.

8

"Hand over that cookie and no one gets hurt!"
I told him, but then he turned with a jerk

and made for the fireplace carrying his sack.
Then instinct kicked in and I leaped on his back.

11

Kicking and scratching, we struggled and fought for the last Christmas cookie, the snack we both sought.

My slumbering family, sound asleep in their bed, heard not a peep as I beat Santa's head.

And then I managed to grab for the prize
and I gobbled it up, before his very eyes.

"You'll regret this," he whispered, so no one could hear.
"Don't forget that I come back every year!"

15

"Bring it on," I taunted, as I watched him go.
Then I straightened the room, so no one would know

that I beat Santa out of the last Christmas cookie.
As I drifted to sleep, I thought, "What a rookie!"

18

On Christmas morning my kids ripped and tore through all of the presents. Then my son said, "One more!

"Hey Mom, it's for you." And they all waited to see as I unwrapped a strange gift there under the tree.

19

As I lifted my gift they looked on with wide eyes.
A pair of red boxing gloves exactly my size.

"Who's it from?" asked my son, scratching his ear.
I smiled. The note said, "I'll see you next year!"

20

# Let's Talk about Writing!

## Learning Questions

1. The style of poetry used to tell the story of *The Last Christmas Cookie* is called a *couplet.* A *couplet* is defined as a complete thought written as two lines with rhyming ends. Can you think of another well-known children's book writer who used *couplets* in his stories? (Hint: he wrote *The Cat in the Hat.*)

2. *Protagonist* is a literary term used to describe the main character of a story. Who do you think is the *protagonist* in *The Last Christmas Cookie*?

3. *Antagonist* is a literary term for a character who deceives, frustrates, or works against the main character in some way. Who is the *antagonist* in *The Last Christmas Cookie*?

4. A *narrator* is the person who tells a story. Who is the *narrator* in *The Last Christmas Cookie*? (Hint: the *narrator* and the *protagonist* are not always the same person, but in *The Last Christmas Cookie* they are.)

5. Sometimes writers like to use a literary device called *hyperbole.* That is when the author exaggerates a situation or statement to make a point, or to be funny. Some people might say the whole

story of *The Last Christmas Cookie* is hyperbole. Why do you think they would say that?

6. *Dialogue* occurs when a conversation takes place between two or more characters. *Dialogue* is written by using quotation marks to indicate the actual words spoken by a character. Can you identify a use of *dialogue* in *The Last Christmas Cookie?*

7. The *setting* of a story is the time, place, and circumstances in which a story takes place. What is the time period of *The Last Christmas Cookie*? What is the place?

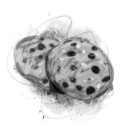

# Let's Talk about the Story!

## Fun-to-Think-About Questions

1. Have you ever woken up in the middle of the night very hungry? What did you do about it?
2. Does your family leave cookies and milk out for Santa on Christmas Eve?
3. Which picture is your favorite in this book?
4. I don't think the Mom in this book was *really* angry with Santa over that cookie, do you? Is it ever right to fight with someone for a cookie?
5. Did you notice anything interesting about the cat in the illustrations of *The Last Christmas Cookie*?
6. What is your favorite kind of cookie?
7. *Gluttonous* is a word you may not have heard before. What do you think it means?
8. What do you think will happen next year when Santa comes back?
9. Did you like this story? Why or why not?

*For more information about*

**The Last Christmas Cookie**

*contact the author, Virginia Smith, at*

*www.VirginiaSmith.org*

## Coming Soon!

## The Last Easter Egg

*by Virginia Smith*

Easter morning is full of sweets, treats, and fun. But what happens when one egg goes missing during the annual Easter egg hunt? Find out in *The Last Easter Egg,* coming soon!

Watch www.NextStepBooks.org for announcements about this and other fun books!

57717423R00020

Made in the USA
Lexington, KY
22 November 2016